Colour
CRACKERS

Read all the Colour CRACKERS books!

A Medal for **Poppy**
The Pluckiest Pig in the World!
Rose Impey and Shoo Rayner

1 84121 244 X

Too Many **Babies**
The Largest Litter in the World!
Rose Impey and Shoo Rayner

1 84121 242 3

Hot Dog **Harris**
The Smallest Dog in the World!
Rose Impey and Shoo Rayner

1 84121 232 6

Rhode Island **Roy**
The Roughest Rooster in the World!
Rose Impey and Shoo Rayner

1 84121 252 0

Welcome Home, **Barney**
The Loneliest Bat in the World!
Rose Impey and Shoo Rayner

1 84121 258 X

Pipe Down, **Prudle!**
The Most Talkative Parrot in the World!
Rose Impey and Shoo Rayner

1 84121 250 4

A Birthday for **Bluebell**
The Oldest Cow in the World!
I'm 78 TODAY!
Rose Impey and Shoo Rayner

1 84121 228 8

1 84121 240 7

1 84121 238 5

1 84121 248 2

1 84121 256 3

1 84121 236 9

1 84121 246 6

1 84121 230 X

1 84121 234 2

1 84121 254 7

Precious Potter

The Heaviest Cat in the World!

Rose Impey
Shoo Rayner

ORCHARD BOOKS

ORCHARD BOOKS
96 Leonard Street, London EC2A 4XD
Orchard Books Australia
Unit 31/56 O'Riordan Street, Alexandria, NSW 2015
First published in Great Britain in 1994
This edition published in hardback in 2002
This edition published in paperback in 2003
Text © Rose Impey 1994
Illustrations © Shoo Rayner 2002
The rights of Rose Impey to be identified as the author
and Shoo Rayner as the illustrator of this work
have been asserted by them in accordance with the
Copyright, Designs and Patents Act, 1988.
A CIP catalogue record for this book is
available from the British Library.
ISBN 1 84121 868 5 (hardback)
ISBN 1 84121 236 9 (paperback)
1 3 5 7 9 10 8 6 4 2 (hardback)
3 5 7 9 10 8 6 4 (paperback)
Printed in China

Precious Potter

In Mrs Potter's litter
there were six kittens.
Well...five and a half, actually.

There was Prudence.

There was Prince

and Princess.

And there were the twins,
Pud and Pod.
That makes five.

And then there was a half.
More like a quarter, in fact.
A little scrap of fur called –
Precious.

At first Mrs Potter had to feed
Precious with an eye-dropper.

She wrapped him in a hanky.

She kept him in a box.

"That kitten will never do any good,"
said his father.
But Mrs Potter said,
"One day this cat will be famous.
You wait and see."

All her neighbours laughed –
behind their paws.

Every day Mrs Potter fed Precious
tiny little mouthfuls
with a tiny little spoon.
She called him her
tiny little sweetheart.

Soon Precious was big enough
to come out of the box
and join his brothers and sisters.
But they didn't want to play
with Precious.

Mrs Potter went on feeding Precious.
A little bit of this

and a little bit of that.

To fatten up her *little cupcake*.
Precious ate everything she gave him.
He ate and ate and ate.

In no time, Precious was as big as
his brothers and sisters.
And his appetite was growing.
When Mrs Potter put out
their bowl of food,
Precious ate as much as the rest.

But Mrs Potter went on
feeding Precious extra little titbits.
Because he had been
such a *poor little scrap,*
to begin with.

By now Precious was eating so much
the other kittens couldn't get their
share of the food.
Prudence said to her mother,
"Ma, I'm hungry.
Precious is eating everything."

But Mrs Potter ignored Prudence.
"Is my little sugar plum hungry?"
she said.

And she put out
a little plate of nibbles
for her *little treasure* to nibble.

Precious nibbled

and nibbled

and nibbled.

So Prudence packed her bag and left.
But Precious was too busy eating
to notice.

Soon Precious was eating so much
Mrs Potter had to make
two bowls of food.
One for Precious
and one for the other kittens.

But the minute she turned her back
Precious ate both.

Whenever Prince and Princess
tried to get near the bowl,
Precious put out his paw
and sent them flying.
"Oh, Ma," they cried.
"Precious is such a pig!"

Mrs Potter just shook her head
and stroked Precious gently.
She said, "My little Swiss roll
has such a good appetite."

Prince and Princess packed a picnic
and left.

But Precious was too busy eating
to notice.

Precious grew bigger and bigger.
No matter how much he ate
he still felt hungry.
Even after two bowls of food,
Precious was looking round
for a little something,
to fill the corners.

Precious looked at Pud and Pod.

He licked his lips

and rolled his eyes.

Pud and Pod picked up their paws
and headed off.
"More for me," thought Precious.

At last Mr Potter noticed
how big Precious had grown.
And how much he was eating.
"Don't you think this kitten
is getting too big?" he said.

"Too big? My little marshmallow?"
said Mrs Potter. "Not at all.
In fact, I think he might need
a little more to eat."

Precious rolled
his little eyes

and licked his
little lips

and looked at Mr Potter's plate.

Mrs Potter gave Precious
his father's dinner.
Mr Potter thought
it was time to go.
Precious didn't mind.
"Just me and Ma now," he thought.

Precious had grown so big
and was so heavy
he had to have a special chair
and a special bowl

and a special bed to sleep in.

Mrs Potter could hardly afford
to feed him.

Soon there was nothing left.
Mrs Potter didn't know what to do.

"You must send Precious out
to work," said her neighbour.
"But he's such a little baby,"
said Mrs Potter.

"He's a great big lump,"
thought her neighbour.
"Anyway, if you don't,"
she said, "you'll both starve."
Mrs Potter couldn't argue with that.

So the next day
she sent Precious out to find a job.
Precious wasn't used to working.

He wasn't used to walking either.
Very slowly he walked through the
town looking for a job.

But Precious was too big
and too heavy for most jobs.
He was too heavy to be a postman.

He was too heavy to clean windows.

He was too heavy to drive a crane.

He was too heavy to fly a plane.

And he was far too heavy
to be a coal miner.

It seemed as if nobody
would give Precious a job.
Precious sat down
at the side of the road.
He was feeling very fed up.
What would he tell his ma
when he went home?

Just then someone came along
and said to Precious,
"May I introduce myself?
I am Freddy Funster.
I am the owner of
Funster's Family Circus."

Are you looking
for a job?

"It's no use," said Precious.
"I am far too big and heavy.
There is nothing I can do."
"Oh, no, you are wrong,"
said Freddy Funster.
"In my circus there is
the perfect job for you."
Precious liked the sound of that.

"What will you pay me?"
asked Precious.
"As much as you can eat,"
said the circus owner.
Precious liked the sound of that too.

So Precious joined
The Funster Family Circus as
"The Heaviest Cat in the World".

Precious
Potter
THE HEAVIEST
CAT IN THE
WORLD

Mrs Potter was so proud of
her *little candy floss.*
"I always knew that cat
would be famous," she said.
This time none of her neighbours
laughed behind their paws.
They clapped their paws instead.

Precious Potter,
"The Heaviest Cat in the World",
ate and ate and ate
and grew bigger and bigger
and bigger…
But Mrs Potter still called him
her *little angel delight.*

Crack-A-Joke

What do you call a cat
that's just eaten a duck?
A duck-filled fatty puss!

Did you hear about the cat that
swallowed a ball of wool?
She had mittens!

What has a head like a cat, feet like a
cat, a tail like a cat, but isn't a cat?
A kitten!

The cat's whiskers!

What do you call a cat with eight legs?
An octopuss!

There are 16 Colour Crackers books.
Collect them all!

❏ A Birthday for Bluebell	1 84121 228 8	£3.99
❏ A Fortune for Yo-Yo	1 84121 230 X	£3.99
❏ A Medal for Poppy	1 84121 244 X	£3.99
❏ Hot Dog Harris	1 84121 232 6	£3.99
❏ Long Live Roberto	1 84121 246 6	£3.99
❏ Open Wide, Wilbur	1 84121 248 2	£3.99
❏ Phew, Sidney!	1 84121 234 2	£3.99
❏ Pipe Down, Prudle!	1 84121 250 4	£3.99
❏ Precious Potter	1 84121 236 9	£3.99
❏ Rhode Island Roy	1 84121 252 0	£3.99
❏ Sleepy Sammy	1 84121 238 5	£3.99
❏ Stella's Staying Put	1 84121 254 7	£3.99
❏ Tiny Tim	1 84121 240 7	£3.99
❏ Too Many Babies	1 84121 242 3	£3.99
❏ We Want William!	1 84121 256 3	£3.99
❏ Welcome Home, Barney	1 84121 258 X	£3.99

Colour Crackers are available from all good bookshops,
or can be ordered direct from the publisher:
Orchard Books, PO BOX 29, Douglas IM99 1BQ
Credit card orders please telephone 01624 836000 or fax 01624 837033
or e-mail: bookshop@enterprise.net for details.
To order please quote title, author and ISBN and your full name and address.
Cheques and postal orders should be made payable to 'Bookpost plc'.
Postage and packing is FREE within the UK
(overseas customers should add £1.00 per book).
Prices and availability are subject to change.

1 84121 244 X

1 84121 240 7

1 84121 238 5

1 84121 252 0

1 84121 256 3

1 84121 236 9

1 84121 228 8

1 84121 230 X

1 84121 234 2

1 84121 248 2

1 84121 242 3

1 84121 232 6

1 84121 246 6

1 84121 258 X

1 84121 250 4

1 84121 254 7

Read all the Colour CRACKERS books!

Collect all the
Colour Crackers!